SCOOBY-DOO MOVIE

ULTIMATE JOKE BOOK

By T. E. J. Dow
AND Howie Dewin

SCHOLASTIC INC.

New York   Toronto   London   Auckland   Sydney
Mexico City   New Delhi   Hong Kong   Buenos Aires

No part of this publication may be reproduced in whole or in part, or stored in a retrieval system, or transmitted in any form or by any means, electronic, mechanical, photocopying, recording, or otherwise, without written permission of the publisher. For information regarding permission, write to Scholastic Inc., Attention: Permissions Department, 557 Broadway, New York, NY 10012.

ISBN 0-439-46820-5

Published by Scholastic Inc. All rights reserved.
SCHOLASTIC and associated logos are trademarks and/or registered trademarks of Scholastic Inc.

Designed by Kay Petronio

12 11 10 9 8 7 6 5 4 3 2 1   2 3 4 5 6/0

Printed in the U.S.A.
First Scholastic printing, October 2002

"Finally! A day just to enjoy ourselves on Spooky Island!" Fred exclaimed.

"Yeah, Far out!" Shaggy agreed. "Like being a movie star is cool, but I'm beat!"

"Uh-oh! — don't look now, but here comes Bobo the Jester!" said Daphne.

"Ruh-roh!" Scooby cried.

Velma shook her head. "That guy never shuts up.

The gang looked at one another. "Run!" they all shouted together.

Just then, Bobo appeared on the scene and began telling jokes:

What is the best thing to take into the desert?

A thirst-aid kit!

> *Run, Shaggy! Bobo's gonna tell you a joke!*

What did the tie say to the hat?

You go on ahead and I'll hang around!

Why did the lazy man want a job in a bakery?

So he could loaf around!

What is it with this place? No matter what we do, somebody ends up getting possessed!

Oh, no! Shaggy's been possessed! He's a goner now.

What is the quickest way to double your money?

Fold it in half.

Whatever! All I know is that it's dangerous to hear this many bad jokes! Run!

Where do hamsters come from?

Hampsterdam!

Where do snowmen go to dance?

A snowball!

What is a cat's favorite TV show?

The evening mews!

What gets lost every time the Shagmeister stands up?

His lap!

What does the Shagman take off last before he goes to bed at night?

His feet off the floor.

What did the mayonnaise say to the refrigerator?

Close the door. I'm dressing.

Why did Shaggy throw the clock out the window?

He wanted to watch time fly, of course!

What did the judge say when Shaggy cut the cheese?

Odor in the court!

What goes up when the rain comes down?

An umbrella.

Why is the Shagster so cool?

He has lots of fans.

When do guys like me take a bubble bath?

After we eat beans for dinner.

That's amazing! Even when he's possessed by Bobo the Jester, Shaggy still talks about nothing but food!

What do sweet potatoes wear to bed?

Their yammies!

What do kittens like to put on their hamburgers?

Catsup!

Why did Shaggy bring Band-Aids to the picnic?

'Cause, like, he heard there were going to be cold cuts, man!

When is Scooby a bad cook?

When he beats an egg.

What kind of dog has no tail?

A hot dog!

What kind of dog has a forked tail?

A devil dog.

Roh rother!

What vegetable do you get when Scooby runs through your garden?

Squash!

Why did Scooby eat the flashbulb?

He wanted a light snack.

Look out, Bobo's coming! Whatever you do, don't answer him!

Shaggy told Scooby that he kept seeing huge juicy veggieburgers in front of his eyes.

Scooby asked Shaggy, "Rave you seen the roctor?"

And Shaggy told him, "No. So far just veggieburgers."

What do you get when you cross, like, a space alien with a crybaby?

An unidentified crying object.

Why didn't the skeleton go to the party?

He had no body to go with!

What happened at the cannibal's wedding party?

They toasted the bride and groom!

Knock-knock.

Who's there?

Turnip.

Turnip who?

Turnip the volume. It's my favorite song!

Knock-knock.

Who's there?

Ben.

Ben who?

Ben to Spooky Island lately?

Knock-knock.

Who's there?

Ken.

Ken who?

Ken you please help me get off of Spooky Island?

Knock-knock.

Who's there?

Acme.

Acme who?

Acme again and I'll tell you!

Knock-knock.

Who's there?

Alex.

Alex who?

Alex plain later.

Knock-knock.

Who's there?

Alfreda.

Alfreda who?

Alfreda the d-d-dark, Scoob?

Knock-knock.

Who's there?

Anita.

Anita who?

Anita p-p-pepperoni p-p-pizza right away!

Knock-knock.

Who's there?

Midas.

Midas who?

Midas well confess, Scooby. I saw you eat the last five Scooby Snacks!

Knock-knock.

Who's there?

Osborne.

Osborne who?

Osborne in Coolsville, USA. How 'bout you?

Knock-knock.

Who's there?

Canoe.

Canoe who?

Canoe imagine a whole boatload of Scooby Snacks just for us?

Knock-knock.

Who's there?

Eel.

Eel who?

Eel kill me if I tell another knock-knock joke!

Knock-knock.

Who's there?

Howie.

Howie who?

Howie going to find those Scooby Snacks, Daphne?

Just be sure not to say "who's there?"!

Uh-oh! He got her! Looks like it's Daphne's turn!

What did the hopeless romantic say to the photographer?

Someday my prints will come.

Why did the frog go to the mall?

To do her summer clothes hopping.

What do you do with a guy like Fred who thinks he's a gift to women?

Exchange him.

Why did the bee join the rock band?

To be the lead stinger.

Why did the musician put strawberries in his guitar?

He wanted to have a jam session.

What kind of music do mummies like?

Wrap!

What kind of instrument does an invisible ghoul play?

Air guitar!

What happens if you sing country music backward?

You get your job and your wife back.

How do you know when a drum solo's really bad?

The bass player notices.

What do a viola and a lawsuit have in common?

Everyone is happy when the case is closed.

Why did the sun worshipper take a vacation?

She was burned out.

Why did the bone doctor take a vacation?

He needed a break.

I need a break from jokes like these!

Why did the bungee jumper take a vacation?

She was at the end of her rope.

Why did the ghost take a vacation?

He was tired of looking pale.

When does Mystery, Inc. go on vacation?

When they get a break in a case.

Why do bellhops like elephants?

They carry their own trunks.

What kind of camp do janitors go to?

Sweep-away camp.

What do you send a witch at camp?

A scare package!

Want to know the best present I ever got?

A harmonica — because my mom gives me extra pocket money every week not to play it!

What lies at the bottom of the sea and shivers?

A nervous wreck!

Uh-oh! It's Fred's turn!

Did you hear about the man who smelled bad on half of his body?

He bought Right Guard, but couldn't find any Left Guard!

Hey, Daphne! Wait up! Remember the time I took you to your first football game? I asked you how you liked the game, and you said, "I like it, but why are they killing each other over a measly 25 cents?"
"What do you mean?" I asked. And you said, "Well, everyone keeps yelling, 'Get the quarter back!'"

Oh, this is going to be bad!

What do you call a monster who flies a kite in a lightning storm?

Benjamin Franklinstein.

Why should you be careful playing against a team of big cats?

They might be cheetahs!

What does a ghost eat for breakfast?

Scream of Wheat!

How did the basketball court get wet?

The players dribbled all over it!

Why did the chicken get sent off the football field?

For persistent fowl play!

Psst. Daphne! Follow us. We'll lose 'im at Dead Mike's Bar & Grill!

Where do football directors go when they are fed up?

The bored room!

Why didn't the dog want to play football?

It was a boxer!

Why does Shaggy always do the backstroke?

Because he's just eaten and he doesn't like to swim on a full stomach!

Daphne

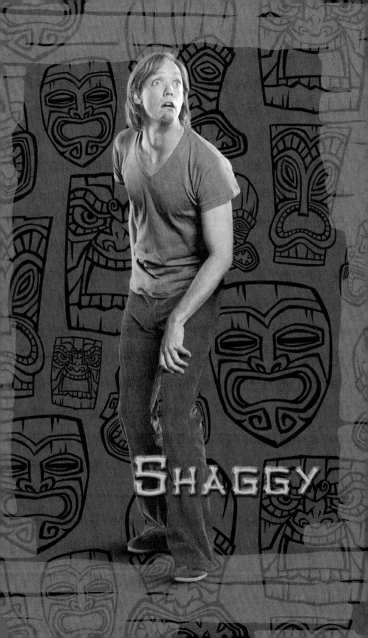

What do you say to a girl who looks really silly in her earmuffs?

Anything you want. She can't hear you.

How do guys like Shaggy sort their laundry?

"Dirty" and "dirty but wearable."

Why did Voodoo Maestro cross the road?

To get to the dead chicken.

Why did the traveler bring a hammer on vacation?

He wanted to hit the road.

Did you hear about the private beach?

It's so exclusive even the tide can't get in.

What makes the leaning Tower of Pisa lean?

It doesn't eat much!

Why is Alabama the smartest state in the U.S.A.?

Because it has four A's and one B!

What is green and has four legs and two trunks?

Two seasick freshmen!

What is the most slippery country in the world?

Greece!

What kind of test do you give a cork?

A pop quiz.

What would you get if you crossed a vampire with a teacher?

Lots of blood tests!

What's the worst thing you're likely to find in the school cafeteria?

The food!

Why did the teacher put the lights on?

Because the class was so dim.

What's the difference between a teacher and a train?

The teacher says "Get that gum out of your mouth," the train says "Chew, chew."

And now for a little bit of history . . .

How did the Vikings send secret messages?

By Norse code!

Who invented King Arthur's round table?

Sir Circumference!

FRED'S THIRD FAVORITE HISTORY JOKE:

What's a forum?

Two-um plus two-um!

Oh, no — looks like it's Velma's turn to be possessed! This should be interesting . . .

Why did the bald man put a rabbit on his head?

He needed the hare.

What does one star say to another star when they meet?

Glad to meteor!

What did the apple say to the worm?

You're boring me.

Why don't oysters give to charity?

Because they're shellfish.

What do you call a dizzy demon?

A wobblin' goblin.

What do you call a monster's oatmeal?

Ghoul gruel.

What do you call a know-it-all?

Fred!

How do you amuse Fred Jones for hours on end?

Write "Please turn over" on both sides of a piece of paper.

How does Fred Jones change a lightbulb?

He holds it in the air and lets the world revolve around him.

Why does Fred carry an umbrella?

To be prepared in the event of a brainstorm!

What is Fred's favorite game?

Follow the leader!

Why does Fred wear two hats when he goes to play miniature golf?

Someone told him he might get a hole in one.

What did Fred say when he saw the elephants coming down the path?

Here come the elephants.

Could someone else please get possessed? I'm tired of Velma's jokes!

What did Fred say when he saw the elephants coming down the path wearing sunglasses?

Nothing. He didn't recognize them.

Okay — how about some brainteasers? Those shouldn't tease Fred at all!

Mr. Jinkleheimer lives on the 37th floor and has a nine-to-five job that takes him 45 minutes to get to. Every morning at 8:15 a.m. he leaves his apartment, waits for the elevator in the hall, gets in the elevator, pushes the button for the lobby, gets out of the elevator, exits the building, and goes to work. When he returns from work in the afternoon he enters his apartment building, pushes the button to call the elevator, gets in the elevator, pushes the button to the 22nd floor, gets out on the 22nd floor and climbs the stairs the rest of the way to his apartment on the 37th floor. Why doesn't Mr. Jinkleheimer ride the elevator right to the 37th floor after work?

Mr. Jinkleheimer is a midget and cannot reach the button to the 37th floor. The highest button that he can reach is for the 22nd floor, so he must use the stairs for the remaining 15 stories.

Leslie and Lorna have the same parents. Leslie and Lorna look exactly like. Leslie and Lorna are the same age, yet they are not twins. How is this possible?

Leslie and Lorna are two members of a set of triplets.

What question can a person ask all day long, always get completely different answers — yet all the answers could be correct?

What time is it?

When the day after tomorrow is yesterday, today will be as far from Tuesday as
today was from Tuesday when the day
before yesterday was tomorrow. What day
is it?

Tuesday.

You have a glass filled up to the top. You
hold it straight out in front of you and you
let it fall to the floor. Is it possible for the
glass to fall without spilling any water?

You won't spill any water if the glass is
filled with milk!

After a man had been blindfolded, someone
hung up his hat. The man walked 100
yards, turned around, and shot a bullet
through his hat. How is such a feat possible?

The hat was hung on the barrel of his rifle.

A woman goes into a pet store to purchase a mynah bird. The man selling the bird tells the woman, "I guarantee that this bird will repeat every word it hears." Ten days later, the woman takes the mynah bird back to the pet shop.

"I want my money back," she says. "This bird doesn't repeat anything. In fact, it doesn't speak at all. Why did you lie to me?"

"Ah, madam," the salesman says. "I swear I did not lie to you."

And that is the truth. The salesman did not lie to the lady. How is that possible?

The mynah bird was deaf, so it didn't hear any words at all.

A farmer had 35 cows. All but 10 died. How many did he have left?

Since all but 10 died, the farmer would have 10 cows left.

How can you drop an uncooked egg five feet without breaking it?

Standing on a tall ladder, drop the egg from a height of 8 feet. After falling 5 feet through the air, the egg will still be quite intact — not actually breaking until it hits the floor, of course.

Ruh?

What do you get if you drop a white hat into the Red Sea?

A wet hat.

How many balls of string would it take to reach the moon?

Just one, but it would have to be a really big one.

When camping out on Spooky Island, what's the best way to make a fire with two sticks?

Make sure one is a match!

What can turn without moving?

Milk can turn sour without moving.

What goes farther the slower it goes?

Money.

Do fish bite at sunrise?

No. Fish bite at worms.

What does a farmer grow if he works day and night?

Tired.

What building has the most stories?

The library.

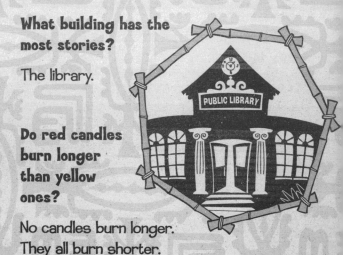

Do red candles burn longer than yellow ones?

No candles burn longer. They all burn shorter.

What should you keep after you give it to someone else?

Your word.

What gets wetter and wetter the more it dries?

A towel gets wetter and wetter the more it dries people's hands.

What is the best way to make a pair of pants last?

Make the coat and vest first.

What divides by uniting and unites by dividing?

A pair of scissors!

Which is faster – heat or cold?

Heat is faster. Anyone can catch cold.

What can you see in the water that never gets wet?

Your reflection.

Can you name something that has to be bad before people consider it good?

Gossip.

How can you make a slow horse fast?

Don't give it anything to eat.

HEY, SCOOBY!

"And now — oh, no! The movie's real star is possessed by the spirit of Bobo!"

Aughroo?

What is the easiest thing to make for dinner?

Reservations!

Scooby Snacks?

What is a Great Dane after he's only four days old?

Five days old.

What dog keeps the best time?

A watch rog.

Where does Scooby leave the Mystery Machine?

In a barking lot.

Where would Scooby go if he rost his tail?

A re-tail store.

How does a puppy row a boat?

With a dog paddle.

What's Scooby's favorite hotel?

The Howliday Inn!

Why don't dogs like to get on the scale?

Recause they hate dog pounds!

What's Scooby's favorite kind of greeting card?

Scratch 'n' Sniff!

What's Scooby's favorite fast breakfast food?

Pup Tarts!

What do giraffes have that other animals don't have?

Little giraffes.

Why do birds fly south for the winter?

The train takes too long.

What time is it when an elephant sits on your fence?

Time to get a new fence.

Hey, Fred, Daphne, Shaggy . . . Shhh . . . follow me to the harbor. I've got a plan!

What kind of animal jumps higher than a house?

All kinds. Houses can't jump.

How many lions can you put in an empty cage?

One. After that the cage isn't empty.

What makes more noise than a cat stuck in a tree?

Two cats stuck in a tree.

What has a head like a cat, a tail like a cat, but isn't a cat?

A kitten.

Who always goes to bed with his shoes on?

A horse.

Why does a stork always stand on one leg?

If he took two legs off the ground, he'd fall down.

Hey, did you hear the one about the giant mosquito?

Never mind. It's over your head!

What do you call a ghoul who loves to entertain?

The ghostess with the mostest.

What did one ghost say to another?

Get real!

Where do you tell a three hundred pound monster to go during summer vacation?

On a diet.

Why is it hard for a ghost to tell a lie?

You can see right through him.

Why did the ghoul get an answering machine?

He likes to scream his calls.

Why did the monster have an upset stomach?

He ate something that disagreed with him.

What do you get when you cross Shaggy with a vampire?

A really ghoul dude!

What do vampires have at eleven o'clock every day?

A coffin break.

Why does Dracula have no friends?

He's a pain in the neck!

What time is it when Fred, Velma, Daphne, Shaggy, and Scooby chase a ghoul?

Five after one.

What's as big as Scooby but weighs nothing at all?

His shadow.

What does Scooby have when he's really sick?

Scooby-Flu.

What do you hear when you cross Scooby with a cow?

Scooby-Moo.

What do you call a really good friend who sticks with you?

Scooby-Glue.

What do you say when you want Scooby to get lost?

Scooby-Shoo!

What do you say when you want to scare Scooby?

Scooby-Boo!

What do you get when you cross Scooby with a dozen eggs?

Pooched eggs!

What do you call a cat with eight legs that likes to swim?

An octopuss!

Doctor, doctor! I swallowed a bone.

Are you choking?

No, I really did!

Doctor, doctor! My son has swallowed my pen. What should I do?

Use a pencil till I get there!

What happened to the naughtly little witch at school?

She was ex-spelled!

What happened when the wizard met the witch?

It was love at first fright!

Did you hear about the cat who swallowed a ball of yarn?

She had mittens!

"I don't think I can take any more of this!" cried Daphne.

"Okay gang, we've got to get out of here," Fred declared. "Here's the plan —"

"Like, oh, no!" interrupted Shaggy. "Here comes Bobo!"

"Not again." Fred groaned.

Velma looked at everyone. "Run! Toward the harbor! We've got to get off this island — now!"

Fred, Daphne, and Velma started running. Shaggy was behind them. "But wait," he called. "What about Scooby?"

What's the best way to keep Scooby from smelling?

Hold his nose!

"Grab him, Shaggy!" Velma cried.

Shaggy grabbed his buddy, and they all raced toward the boat that would take them back to shore.

"Whew!" the gang all cried at once.

Shaggy turned to his friends. "I just have one last joke—"

"Oh, no!" they groaned.

What do you call a long story on a boat ride?

A ferry tale!

Scooby-Doo Ya Get it?